This book belongs to:

. . . .

To the memory of Florrie.
And for Paul, with love and thanks,
for believing and being there.

First published in Great Britain 1998
This edition published 2003
by Egmont Books Limited
239 Kensington High Street, London W8 6SA

1 3 5 7 9 10 8 6 4 2

Text and illustrations copyright © Jan Fearnley 1998
Jan Fearnley has asserted her moral rights
A CIP catalogue record for this title is available from The British Library

ISBN 1 4052 0845 7

Printed in Italy

Little Robin Red Vest

by

Jan Fearnley

EGMONT

It was the week before Christmas and Little Robin was getting very excited. He washed and ironed seven warm vests for the frosty days ahead.

He put on his white vest
and set out to skate on the pond.
On the way, he met Frog.
"I'm so cold!" said Frog. "Can you help?"

Little Robin gave Frog his white vest.
"I've still got six vests left," he thought,
as Frog hopped off happily.

Six days before Christmas, Little Robin put
on his green vest and dashed out to play in the snow.
Down the path came Hedgehog.
"I'm freezing!" he said.

Little Robin gave Hedgehog his green vest.
"I've still got five vests left," he thought,
waving goodbye to his prickly friend.

Five days before Christmas, Little Robin put on his
pink vest, and went to look for worms.

He hadn't gone far when Mole appeared.
"Brrrrrrr! The ground's too hard to dig,
and I'm chilly," he complained.

So Little Robin gave his pink vest to Mole.
It was a bit tight, but Mole didn't mind.
He was nice and warm.
"Four vests left," thought Little Robin.

Four days before Christmas, Little Robin
put on his yellow vest and flew up to sit in the
tall oak tree where he met Squirrel.
"I'm so cold I can't sleep!"
Squirrel grumbled.

Little Robin handed over his yellow vest.
"Only three vests left now," he thought,
as Squirrel dozed off.

Three days before Christmas,
Little Robin put on his blue vest.

He was swooping
down through the clouds
when he saw Rabbit on the hill.
"I'm so cold my teeth are chattering!"
shivered Rabbit.

Little Robin gave Rabbit his blue vest.
"Well, I've still got two left," he said to himself,
as Rabbit went cheerfully on his way.
Two days before Christmas, Little Robin put on his
purple vest and skipped along the river bank.

Next to the river stood Otter with her baby.
She was very unhappy. "My baby is poorly!" she said.

Little Robin's purple vest was just right for
Baby Otter, and made him feel much better.
"Oh dear, I've only one vest left," thought Little Robin.

On the day before Christmas, Little Robin
put on his very last vest, a warm, orange one.
He'd been walking and whistling to himself for
some time when he met a little mouse,
shivering in the garden.

Little Robin felt so sorry for her that he
took off his last woolly vest and pulled
it over her chilly little ears.

Now it was late on Christmas Eve,
the snow was falling and poor Little Robin
had nothing warm to wear. There was nobody
around to help him, and it was a long way home.
He fluffed up his feathers as best he could and
huddled miserably on a snowy roof.

Soon he fell fast asleep.
Not even the sleigh bells
woke him. Or the crunch
of snow under two heavy,
black boots.

Large hands scooped
Little Robin up and
tucked him into a soft
white beard.
"You had better come
with me, my lad!" chuckled
a gruff, jolly voice.

"This is the generous little fellow I told you about,"
the man said to his wife.
"He must have a very special present then," she replied.

And with Little Robin snug and cosy in her lap, the lady
set to work . . . She pulled a thread from a big, bright red
coat, and with it she knitted a tiny vest.
It was a perfect fit for a little bird.

"I'm very proud of you," said the man with a smile.
"You gave away all your warm clothes
to help other people.
You are full of the spirit of Christmas.

Now it's time for your present.
This vest is very, very special. It will keep you warm
forever and, when other people see you, it will make
them feel warm too."

It was time to go, back across the skies
as the sun rose to kiss the land. Little Robin was
very happy. His chest glowed as red as a reindeer's nose.

Soon Little Robin was home. "Merry Christmas!"
cried the man as he flew off.
"Goodbye, and thank you!" Little Robin shouted back.

It was Christmas morning. Boys and girls
everywhere were opening their presents.
Little Robin flew to the highest branch,
proudly wearing his new red vest, and sang out
sweetly to wish everyone a "Merry Christmas!"

**Jan Fearnley has created lots more
books for you to enjoy:**

Mr Wolf's Pancakes
0 7497 3559 7

Mr Wolf and the Three Bears
0 7497 4627 0

A Special Something
0 7497 4639 4

Just Like You
0 7497 4231 3

A Perfect Day For It
1 4052 0176 2

Blue Banana Titles:

Mabel and Max
0 7497 3215 6

Colin and the Curly Claw
0 7497 4646 7